Dirty Bertie

HORROR!

DAVID ROBERTS WRITTEN BY ALAN MACDONALD

stripes

Collect all the
Dirty Bertie books!

Contents

CHAPTER 1

Gran was round at Bertie's house.
She seemed pleased with herself for
some reason.

"Notice anything different?" she said.

"New dress?" asked Dad.

"New shoes?" asked Mum.

"You've got fatter," said Bertie.

"I have not!" snapped Gran. "If you

must know, I've had my hair done."

Bertie stared. It was true. Gran's hair was normally white and frizzy, but today it was blonde and frizzy.

"I wanted to look smart for the cinema," she said.

"The cinema?" cried Bertie. "Can I come?"

"You?" said Gran.

"Yes, they're showing *Return of the Blob Thing*," said Bertie. "Darren says it's meant to be well scary."

"It doesn't sound suitable," said Mum. "Anyway, I'm sure Gran doesn't want to see a scary film."

Gran smiled. "Well, I'd have to ask Reg," she said, blushing a little.

"Reg? Who's Reg?" asked Dad.

"My new boyfriend," giggled Gran.

"Tomorrow's our first date."

Boyfriend? Bertie almost choked on his biscuit. Should Gran be getting a boyfriend at her age? Next she'd be wearing jeans and getting her nose pierced!

"I met him at ballroom dancing," she continued. "He says I'm a lovely mover."

"Does he now?" said Dad. "And he's taking you on a date?"

"That's right," said Gran. "He's quite the charmer. I think he fancies me, Bertie." She burst into a fit of giggles.

Bertie didn't know where to look. What had got into her? Gran wasn't normally like this – she sounded like a fourteen-year-old!

"What were you saying about a film, Bertie?" said Gran.

"Oh no, that's okay," said Bertie quickly. "You go with whatshisname."

The last thing he wanted was a cinema trip with Gran and her boyfriend. How embarrassing! What if they held hands during the film? What if they put their arms round each other and… No, he didn't even want to think about it.

While Gran was upstairs in the loo, Dad turned to Bertie. "Maybe you *should* go to the cinema tomorrow," he said.

"Me? No way!" said Bertie.

"But I thought you wanted to go?"

"Not with Gran and her boyfriend!"

Dad sighed. "The problem is, we don't know anything about this Reg," he said. "He could be after her money."

"Really?" said Bertie. He didn't know
Gran had any money!

"What I mean is, he could be
anybody," said Dad. "He might be a
crook … or a kidnapper!"

"Don't be silly," scoffed Mum. "She
met him at ballroom dancing."

"Oh well, that's all right, then!" said
Dad, rolling his eyes. "All I'm saying is,
Bertie could keep an eye on her."

Dirty Bertie

"Why me? If you're so worried, YOU go!" said Bertie.

"I can't go, she's my mother!" said Dad. He brought out his wallet. "Look, how much is the cinema?" he asked. "Here's five pounds."

Bertie hesitated. He would much rather see the film with his friends. But this might be his only chance.

"Can I see *Return of the Blob Thing*?" he asked.

"I don't see why not," said Dad.

"Only if Gran thinks it's suitable," said Mum.

Gran was coming back. "Don't tell her I put you up to this," whispered Dad.

Bertie stuffed the money into his pocket. Result!

CHAPTER 2

"You jammy dodger!" said Darren on the way to school the next day. "How did you fix that?"

Bertie shrugged. "It was easy. Dad's actually paying me to go."

"I wish my mum would let me go," said Eugene. "She says I'm not old enough for scary films."

Dirty Bertie

"My dad says the cinema costs too much," sighed Darren. "Who's taking you, anyway?"

Bertie looked uncomfortable. "Actually it's my gran – and her boyfriend," he admitted.

"HER BOYFRIEND!" Darren burst out laughing. "Ha ha! Seriously?"

"You *are* joking?" said Eugene.

"It'll be fine," said Bertie.

"I wouldn't bet on it," said Darren. "Are they in love?"

"NO!" cried Bertie. "It's the first time they've gone out."

"That's even worse," said Darren. "My mum made my sister and her boyfriend take me to the cinema once. As soon as the lights went down they started, you know … kissing."

Dirty Bertie

"EWW!" cried Eugene.

"This is my gran!" said Bertie. "She's about ninety!"

"Exactly," said Darren. "Imagine seeing your gran kissing in the cinema. Gross!"

Bertie didn't want to imagine it. There was no way he wanted to be there if Gran and her boyfriend were getting all smoochy. He'd be having nightmares about it for months!

Dirty Bertie

If Bertie had his way, old people wouldn't be allowed to go on dates, they'd stick to knitting and bingo. But he'd promised to go now. He'd just have to make sure that Gran and Reg didn't get any ideas.

The next evening, Bertie arrived at Gran's house. As usual Gran hadn't finished getting ready. She was still in her petticoat and fluffy slippers.

She held two dresses against her in turn for him to inspect. "What do you think, Bertie?" she asked. "The green one … or the red? Which goes better with my hair?"

"I don't care!" groaned Bertie, covering his eyes. "Just put something on!"

Gran went off to get changed and put on her make-up. Bertie thought she was going to a lot of trouble for a trip to the cinema.

DING-DONG!

"That'll be Reg," said Gran, hurrying out. "How do I look?"

"At least you're dressed," said Bertie.

Gran opened the front door. Reg was wearing a checked jacket and a yellow scarf knotted round his neck. He'd

Dirty Bertie

tried to hide his bald patch by combing over what was left of his hair. If Gran reckoned he was good looking, she needed her eyes tested, thought Bertie.

"Dotty! Don't you look a picture!" cried Reg, coming in.

Bertie stood there scowling, his arms folded.

"And who's this young man?" asked
Reg.

"This is Bertie, my grandson," said
Gran. "I told you he might be coming."

"Oh. I thought you were joking," said
Reg. He bent down to Bertie's level.
"Wouldn't you rather be with your little
friends?" he asked.

"None of them are allowed to come,"
said Bertie.

"Well, I hope you're going to behave,"
said Reg. "Mind you, I can't promise the
same for me and Dotty."

"Oh stop it, Reg!" hooted Gran.

Bertie rolled his eyes. If they were
going to carry on like this all night, he
might have to wear a bag over his head.

They squeezed into Reg's tiny car
and drove to the cinema. Bertie had

to squash in the back. Reg's aftershave stunk the car out, and he kept looking in the driver's mirror to check his hair. Gran did her best to laugh at his terrible jokes.

At least when the film started Reg would have to shut up, thought Bertie.

CHAPTER 3

There was a long queue at the box office when they arrived. The multiplex was showing eight films on different screens.

"Can I get some popcorn?" asked Bertie. "And a slushy?"

"Go on then," said Gran.

"My treat," said Reg. "Take your time, we'll be in the queue."

Dirty Bertie

Bertie hurried off. He chose the Giant Whopper popcorn that came in a huge bucket, and a bright red strawberry slushy. He carried them across the foyer, spilling popcorn as he went. On the way he spotted a poster.

RETURN OF THE BLOB THING

IT'S BACK... AND EVEN BLOBBIER!

NOW SHOWING ON SCREEN 4

Bertie couldn't wait. He hurried back to join Gran and Reg.

"It's showing on Screen 4," he told them, excitedly.

"What is?" asked Gran.

"The film, of course... *Return of the Blob Thing*," said Bertie.

"You're too late," said Reg. "We've just bought tickets for this one."

He pointed at a poster above them. The film was called *Me, You and Bonzo Too*. The poster showed a smiling couple cuddling a cute puppy.

Bertie gaped at it. "But that's not the film I want to see," he moaned.

"Well, *we* want to see it," said Reg. "It looks nice."

"And you're a bit young for scary films," said Gran.

Reg patted Bertie on the head. "Never mind, you'll like this one," he said. "It's a love story."

Bertie's shoulders drooped. This was going to be the worst night of his life. Reg probably thought a love story would put Gran in a romantic mood. Well, not if Bertie had anything to do with it.

They went into the cinema. Gran found three seats near the front. Bertie flopped into the seat next to her.

Reg tapped him on the shoulder. "You're in my seat," he grumbled.

"No, I'm not," said Bertie.

"You ARE," said Reg, crossly. "I want to sit next to Dotty."

"Well, so do I," said Bertie. "Why can't you sit in that seat?"

"*You* sit in that one," snapped Reg.

Dirty Bertie

The woman sitting behind them made
a loud tutting noise.

"Just sit down, Reg," sighed Gran.
"People are looking."

Reg sat down in a sulk. Bertie sucked
his slushy drink. There wouldn't be any
lovey-dovey stuff with him sitting in the
middle. Gran and Reg would just have
to watch the film.

The lights went down as the film
began.

Dirty Bertie

CRUNCH, CRUNCH!
SLUUUURP, SLUUUURP!
A hand tapped Bertie on the shoulder. It was the woman sitting behind them. "Do you have to make that noise?" she grumbled.

"It's popcorn, I can't help it," replied Bertie.

"Well, if you must eat, do it QUIETLY," hissed the woman.

Dirty Bertie

Gran gave Bertie a look. Bertie sighed. How were you meant to eat popcorn quietly? This was no fun – and the film looked rubbish. The man and woman were on a beach with the cute puppy scampering around.

"I love you," sighed the man.

"I love you too," cooed the woman.

"Woof! Woof!" barked the cute puppy.

Bertie wished the Blob Thing would appear and gobble them up. Suddenly he had a brilliant idea. What was to stop him sneaking off to see *Return of the Blob Thing*? It was showing next door. Gran and Reg were so caught up in the film, they wouldn't even notice he'd gone.

He stood up.

"Just off to the toilet," he said.

CHAPTER 4

Bertie peeped through the door. The coast was clear. He crept into the cinema and slid into a seat on the back row. His plan had worked perfectly. Now he could sit back and enjoy the scariest film ever.

On the screen it was night time. A woman jumped into a car and locked the doors. She was trying to escape, but the car wouldn't start.

SHLOOP! SHLOOP! Something slimy was moving in the woods.

BANG! Suddenly the car shook.

Bertie hid his eyes. He couldn't look – the Blob Thing was coming…

ARGHHH! THERE IT WAS!

Bertie jumped out of his seat and fled for the door…

Back next door, Bertie clambered over people's legs to get to his seat.

"What took you so long?" Gran whispered.

"I got lost!" said Bertie.

He went to sit down – but wait, what was this? Reg had pinched his seat!

"You're in my seat!" hissed Bertie.

"It's my seat now," replied Reg. "Sit there."

"Will you just sit down and BE QUIET!" snapped the woman behind them.

Bertie sat down next to Reg, who shot him a look of triumph.

Okay, you asked for it, thought Bertie. *This is war.*

Dirty Bertie

In the film the couple were huddled on
the sofa with the puppy. Reg pretended
to yawn. His arm crept round Gran's
shoulder. He snuggled in closer. Bertie
remembered what Darren had said
about his sister and her boyfriend. He
had to do something quickly. He smiled
to himself. Maybe some strawberry
slushy would cool things down?

Dirty Bertie

Bertie leaned across. "Anyone want a drink?" he asked.

"Ugh! No, take it away!" said Reg, pushing Bertie's hand away.

Oops! Ice-cold strawberry slushy emptied into Reg's lap. He shot to his feet as if he'd been stung.

"YEEAARGHHHH!" he cried.

"Bertie!" groaned Gran.

"You idiot!" snarled Reg.

"It wasn't my fault!" said Bertie.

"RIGHT, THAT'S IT! I'm calling the manager!" cried the woman sitting in the row behind.

Bertie never got to see the end of *Me, You and Bonzo Too* because the manager asked them to leave. Bertie could guess what happened anyway. They got married and lived happily ever after.

Reg wasn't so happy. He drove them home in stony silence and parked outside Gran's door.

"Well, thank you, Reg," said Gran. "How are your trousers now?"

"Damp," said Reg stiffly. "I won't come in, thank you."

"Perhaps it's for the best," said Gran.

Bertie got out and waited on the pavement.

Reg sniffed. "I won't be at ballroom dancing next week, I'm taking Beryl out to dinner," he said. "Just the *two* of us."

"I see," said Gran. She got out and slammed the car door.

Bertie and Gran watched Reg drive off.

"Ah well," sighed Gran. "I was going off him anyway. I think he fancies himself."

"Yes," agreed Bertie. "He smells of cat wee too."

Gran laughed. "I think that's his aftershave," she said. "Come on, I've got some chocolate cake in the cupboard."

Bertie followed her indoors. He felt in

his pocket. Actually, the evening hadn't been a total disaster. Gran had bought his ticket so he still had the five pounds Dad had given him. And next week at the cinema they were showing *Pirates of Blood Island 3*…

CHAPTER 1

Miss Boot seemed to be in a good mood this morning.

"I have some exciting news," she said. "Next Tuesday we are all going on a school trip."

Bertie sat up. He loved going on trips. The coach ride, the crisps and fizzy drinks, the being sick on the way home... Last term they'd gone to the zoo, which had been brilliant – apart from getting his head stuck in the bars of a monkey cage. But where was Miss Boot planning to take them this time? Maybe to the Space Centre – or, better still, to Chocolate World!

"You'll be excited to hear we are going to the City Art Gallery," said Miss Boot.

"The *art gallery?*" Bertie groaned so loudly that everyone turned round.

"Yes, the art gallery, Bertie," said Miss Boot, icily. "And not just any art. We have the chance to see one of the world's greatest paintings."

She clicked on her laptop and a picture came up. It showed a bunch of flowers in a vase.

"Does anyone know this painting?"
asked Miss Boot. "Who can tell me
what it's called?"

A hand shot up. "It's *Sunflowers*, by
Van Boff," said Nick, smugly.

Trust Know-All Nick to know the answer,
thought Bertie.

"Very good, Nicholas," said Miss
Boot. "This painting belongs to a famous
gallery in London, but next week it's
coming here. You are very lucky to have

the chance to see it."

"Why's it so famous, Miss?" asked Eugene.

"Because Van Boff was a great artist and this is one of his finest paintings," said Miss Boot. "Look at it carefully – the colours, the brushwork – it is a masterpiece."

Bertie looked. Van Boff had certainly used a lot of paint. But why waste it on a bunch of droopy old flowers? If it was Bertie's painting, he'd at least choose something interesting – like a Tyrannosaurus rex fighting an army of ninja robots.

He stuck up his hand. "Is it worth anything?" he asked.

Miss Boot laughed. "It's a Van Boff, Bertie, it's priceless."

"You mean free?"

Dirty Bertie

"I mean, it is worth millions," said Miss Boot.

Millions? Bertie's mouth fell open. People would pay a million pounds for that splodgy old flower painting? Why hadn't anyone told him this before? He'd have paid a lot more attention in art lessons! For a million pounds he'd paint anything – even Nick's ugly face. And what about the doodles inside his maths book? He'd done some great cartoons of Miss Boot. Maybe the art gallery would buy them!

$2 \times 2 = 4$
$2 \times 3 = 6$
$2 \times 4 = 10$
$2 \times 5 =$

Dirty Bertie

Back home, Bertie handed his mum a letter from Miss Boot.

"It's a school trip," he explained. "I was hoping for Chocolate World but it's an art gallery."

"The City Art Gallery?" said Mum. "Well, that could be fun."

"Hmm," said Bertie, helping himself to biscuits. "Miss Boot wants us to see some old flower painting."

"Flower painting?" said Mum. "You don't mean Van Boff's *Sunflowers*?"

"Yes, that's it," said Bertie.

"But that's amazing," said Mum. "I was reading in the local paper that it's coming here. I've always wanted to see it."

Bertie wiped his mouth. "I don't see what the fuss is about, it's only some old picture," he said.

"It's a Van Boff," said Mum. "Do you know what that painting is worth?"

"Miss Boot says millions," replied Bertie.

"Yes, and it's world famous – everyone knows it," said Mum.

"I don't," Bertie said.

"No, but you're going to see it," said Mum. "I wish I was going. You don't know how lucky you are."

Bertie sniffed. Everyone kept telling him how lucky he was, but he'd much rather Miss Boot took them to Chocolate World. They gave away free chocolate bars to every visitor – now *that* would be lucky!

CHAPTER 2

Class 3 filed into the art gallery behind Miss Boot and Mr Weakly. They had arrived early to avoid the crowds.

"Right," said Miss Boot. "Let me remind you that this is an art gallery, not a playground. There'll be no running or fighting and no eating sweets or crisps. Most importantly, I don't want

Dirty Bertie

you TOUCHING. Is that clear, Bertie?"

"Touching what?" asked Bertie.

"Touching *anything*," said Miss Boot.

Bertie sighed heavily. Why did
teachers always pick on him? All he'd
done was get off the coach!

Mr Weakly came round handing out
some worksheets that the gallery had
supplied. Bertie looked around at the
paintings.

"Sir, which is the one that's worth millions?" he asked.

"The Van Boff? Ah, that's in a room by itself," said Mr Weakly. "They're letting us see it later."

Miss Boot split the class into two groups to go round the gallery. Luckily Bertie and his friends were in Mr Weakly's group. Mr Weakly was a nervous young teacher whose speech was peppered with "ahhs", "errs" and "umms". Bertie had never even heard him raise his voice – apart from the time he got locked in the store cupboard.

They wandered round the gallery, looking at the paintings. Bertie stared at a picture of people in big hats having a picnic. It made him hungry. His mum had given him some spending money and on

the way in he'd spotted a gift shop. But
the teachers wouldn't let him near it.
Unless… Bertie had an idea. He pressed
his pencil on to his worksheet.

SNAP!

That should do the trick. Now to ask
Mr Weakly.

"My pencil's broken, sir," complained
Bertie, holding it up.

"Oh dear!" said Mr Weakly. "Don't
you have another one?"

"No," said Bertie.

"Well, ah … surely someone could
lend you one?"

"They can't," said Bertie. "But it's fine,
they sell pencils in the shop."

"Do they? Oh well… Mmm," said Mr
Weakly. He looked round for Miss Boot,
but she was nowhere to be seen.

Dirty Bertie

"I'm not sure we're allowed in the shop yet," he said.

"It's okay, it won't take a minute!" said Bertie. He hurried off before Mr Weakly could say any more. Now what could he buy with his spending money?

Dirty Bertie

"Where have you been?" asked Darren.

Bertie wiped chocolate from round his mouth.

"Gift shop," he said. "And look what I got. It was in the Bargain Bin."

He checked that no teachers were about and pulled something from his pocket.

"A WATER PISTOL!" cried Eugene.

"Shh! Keep your voice down!" hissed Bertie. "It works too. I filled it up in the boys' toilets."

"Better not let Miss Boot see it," said Darren. "She'll go mad."

Bertie looked around for a suitable victim. Now, who could he squirt? Trevor? Royston Rich? Or what about

Dirty Bertie

that sneaky show-off...

"I've finished!" boasted Nick, waving his worksheet. "And I bet I got them all right too."

Dirty Bertie

Perfect timing, thought Bertie. He raised his water pistol and took aim.

Nick gaped at him. "Where did you get that?" he squawked.

"From the shop," smiled Bertie. "Let's see if it works, shall we?"

CHAPTER 3

"HEEEEELP!"

Nick skidded round a corner, panting for breath. Bertie raced after him, the water pistol in his hand.

"Aha! Got you now!" Bertie cried.

The room was empty.

"Keep away!" moaned Nick. "I'll tell Miss Boot!"

"She's not here," said Bertie.

"I'll scream!" wailed Nick.

"Prepare to die," said Bertie, aiming the water pistol. His finger tightened on the trigger.

SQUIRT!

At the last moment Nick ducked under a rail, escaping into a side room.

Rats! Why can't he stay still? thought Bertie. The side room was small and dimly lit. Something stood on an easel partly covered by a pair of red velvet curtains. Nick's face suddenly shot out from behind it.

"CAN'T CATCH ME!" he yelled.

SQUOOOOOOOSH!

Bertie squirted a big jet of water. He missed, hitting the red curtains instead.

Nick crept out from behind the easel.

"Umm, look what you've done!" he said.

Bertie pulled back the curtains. He
gasped. Underneath was a painting he
recognized straight away. Van Boff's
Sunflowers! It was worth millions and
he'd just squirted it. Water had splashed
the curtain and dripped down the
painting, plopping on the floor.

Nick stared, wide-eyed. "You are dead."

Dirty Bertie

"It's only water, it'll come off," said
Bertie. He reached out, dabbing the wet
patch with his sleeve.

"Don't touch it!" warned Nick. But it
was too late. Bertie stared at the smudge
of green paint on his sleeve. He gulped.
This couldn't be happening! If Miss Boot
found out, the art gallery would have him
arrested. His mum and dad would have
to sell the house and probably his sister
to pay the money back.

Nick was backing away, eager to escape. "I'm telling!" he said.

"You can't!" begged Bertie. "They'll kill me."

"You should have thought of that when you bought a water pistol," said Nick.

"If you tell tales, I'll say it was your fault," said Bertie.

"You wouldn't!"

"Try me."

Nick frowned. He didn't want to risk getting in trouble – and he shouldn't have entered the room in the first place.

"Okay, I won't tell," he said. "But the painting's your problem."

He ducked under the rail and hurried off.

Left alone, Bertie stared at the

smudged, priceless painting. Any
moment now someone might come in
and discover what he'd done. He had
to think fast. Maybe he could hide the
painting? But Mr Weakly said people
were coming in to see it. If only he
could make it look like new.

Bertie's eyes lit up. Of course! It was
only a bunch of droopy flowers in a vase.
Anyone could draw that! All he needed
was paper and Eugene's felt-tip pens. By
the time he'd finished, his picture would
be as good as a Van Boff – probably
even better! But first he had
to hide the real thing.

CHAPTER 4

An hour later, Miss Boot gathered her class together. The great moment had arrived. The art gallery was about to present Van Boff's *Sunflowers* in Room 21.

"Now, follow me," said Miss Boot. "If we hurry, we should get a good view."

They made their way to Room 21,

following people who were heading the same way. Bertie caught Nick's eye and put a finger to his lips. If they both kept their mouths shut maybe they'd come out of this alive.

They filed into the small room, which was already filling up with people. In the centre stood the priceless painting, hidden under the curtains and bathed in a spotlight. The crowd parted to let the class through to the front. Bertie wouldn't have minded staying at the back, in case he needed to make a quick exit.

The director of the gallery stepped forward. Bertie held his breath. This was it – the moment he'd been dreading!

Dirty Bertie

"Well, thank you all for coming," said the director. "This is a very proud day for the City Gallery. It is my pleasure to present one of the world's greatest masterpieces ... Van Boff's *Sunflowers!*"

Dirty Bertie

She pulled on a cord and the red curtains swished back. The crowd gasped. The painting in front of them showed flowers in a vase, but it wasn't a Van Boff. It was a Van Bertie.

The flowers were messy blobs of red and brown drawn in felt-tip pen. They drooped from a vase that looked like a dog bowl. In one corner someone had signed the picture "VAN BIFF" in childish handwriting.

The director stared, holding her head. "Is this some sort of joke?" she said. "Where is the Van Boff?"

Bertie had gone bright red. It didn't look like they had got away with it. The director was phoning someone. Security guards rushed in while everyone talked at once.

Dirty Bertie

Suddenly Miss Boot stepped forward.
"Excuse me," she said. "Do you mind
if I take a closer look?"

She bent over to inspect the blobby
picture. Something about the style was
familiar – the messy colours, the terrible
handwriting. She groaned. Of course –
she might have known!

Van
Biff.

Dirty Bertie

"BERTIE!" boomed Miss Boot. "I want a word with you."

Uh oh, thought Bertie. How did she know it was him?

He trailed out to the front.

"Did you draw this picture, Bertie?" demanded Miss Boot.

"Me?" said Bertie. "N-no!"

"Show me your hands," ordered Miss Boot.

Bertie held them out. He had felt-tip pen on his fingers and paint on his sleeve.

Dirty Bertie

"I'll ask you one last time," said Miss Boot. "Is this your picture?"

"Um…"

"It wasn't my fault!" wailed Know-All Nick. "He chased me with a water pistol!"

Bertie rolled his eyes. Trust Know-All Nick to give the game away.

Miss Boot's eyes blazed. "Where is it, Bertie?" she thundered. "What have you done with the real Van Boff?"

Bertie swallowed hard. "Don't worry," he said. "I've hidden it somewhere really safe."

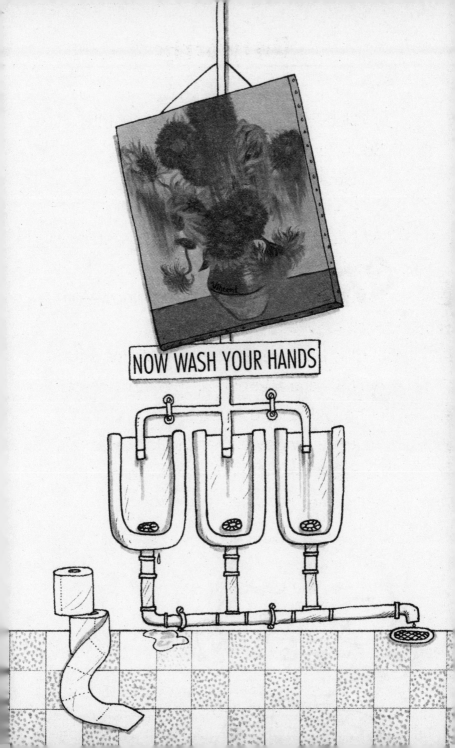

CHAPTER 1

Bertie reached up to grab his money box. There was a pirate telescope he needed to buy. With a telescope he could spy on his enemies and spot Miss Boot coming from a mile away.

He emptied out his cash.

PLINK!

Huh? Five measly pence! How come

he never had any money? It was all right for his mum and dad – they had jobs. When Bertie grew up he was going to get a job that paid a fortune. He'd be a robot scientist or a chocolate taster or maybe King of England. But the trouble was he needed money *now*.

He thought hard. Maybe he *could* get a job. What about Darren's cousin Neil? He had a paper round. If Bertie had a paper round he could buy a hundred telescopes. He'd tell Darren his idea tomorrow.

Neil went to the big school down the road. Bertie and Darren waited for him by the gates at home time.

"This is a brilliant idea," said Darren.

"That's on my round," said Neil.
"Listen, I'll do you a big favour. I'll pay you
a pound to deliver papers to your street
and Hazel Road."

"A pound EACH?" said Darren.

"Do I look stupid?" said Neil. "A
pound between you, that's the deal.
Take it or leave it."

Bertie and Darren stepped aside to
talk it over.

"A pound? It's not very
much," grumbled
Darren.

"But it's better
than nothing,"
said Bertie.
"And with both
of us it wouldn't
take long."

"True," said Darren. "Okay, I'm in."

They told Neil they would do it.

"Great," he said. "I'll come round tomorrow and drop off the papers."

Neil watched them go, smiling to himself. For him it was *definitely* a good deal. He'd got rid of almost half of his paper round and it was only costing him one pound a week. That still left him seven pounds in his pocket. Best of all, he was losing the street that he always dreaded – Hazel Road. *Poor little kids*, he thought, *they've no idea what's in store for them.*

CHAPTER 2

Bertie arrived home and threw his bag down in the hall. He was excited about the paper round, but there was just one small problem. He hadn't actually asked his parents yet.

He found his mum emptying the washing machine.

"Mum," he began. "You know

Darren's cousin?"

"Not really," replied Mum.

"The one with big ears."

"That's half the boys you know," said Mum. "But what about him?"

"He's got us a job!" said Bertie.

Mum stared. "A job? What kind of job?" she asked.

"A paper round," said Bertie. "It's okay, we're getting paid."

"You're telling me a newsagent is paying *you* to deliver papers?" said Mum.

"Not a newsagent, Darren's cousin," said Bertie. He explained the deal they'd made with Neil. Mum frowned.

"What does Darren's mum say about this?" she asked.

"She thinks it's brilliant," said Bertie. At least she would when Darren told her.

"Hmm," said Mum. "I don't want you crossing busy roads."

"We won't have to," said Bertie. "It's only our street and Hazel Road. Anyway, I'll be with Darren."

Mum rolled her eyes. Darren was about as sensible as a chimpanzee.

Still, it might not be such a bad idea.

"Maybe it would do you good to earn some pocket money," said Mum. "You might not spend it so quickly."

"I wouldn't!" said Bertie. "I'm saving up."

Mum sighed. "All right, we'll see how it goes."

"YAY! Thanks!" cried Bertie.

"But don't go any further than Hazel Road," warned Mum.

"We won't," promised Bertie. He dashed off to phone Darren with the good news. Starting tomorrow they were going to be rich!

The next day Neil dropped off a big batch of newspapers at Bertie's house.

Dirty Bertie

Bertie and Darren stared at them.
"There's hundreds," moaned Darren.
"It'll take us forever!"

Dirty Bertie

Bertie looked at his watch. "*Danny's Deadly Dinosaurs* starts in half an hour," he said. It was his favourite programme.

Darren sighed. "We'll never make it back in time."

"We will if we get a move on," said Bertie.

They dumped out books, pens and apple cores from their school bags and divided the newspapers between them. It was a tight fit but they managed it.

Dirty Bertie

They decided to begin on Hazel Road and work back to Bertie's street.

The houses on Hazel Road had long driveways and tall iron gates. At first Bertie found the letterboxes too small, but he soon learned to roll up the newspapers. After a few houses he started to get into his stride. Across the road, he saw that Darren was keeping up. Bertie waved.

"Let's speed up!" he called. "Ten minutes to finish this road."

"Easy," said Darren. "I'm super quick."

"I'm on fire," said Bertie. If they carried on at this speed they'd be back in time to watch *Danny's Deadly Dinosaurs*.

Bertie raced to the next house, pulling a paper from his bag. There was a red car in the driveway. He weaved round it, trampling the flowerbed.

THUNK! The newspaper whizzed through the letterbox. Bertie wheeled away, taking a shortcut across the lawn. Over the road Darren was zooming in and out of driveways like a greyhound. Bertie grabbed a bunch of newspapers and flung open the next gate. A garden gnome went flying as he skidded down the path. THUNK!

At number twenty the garden wall was only knee-high. Bertie cleared it in one go. THUNK! Another paper slammed home. The next wall was bigger, but it was still quicker than taking the drive. He threw over his bag and scrambled after it...

"GRRRRRR!"

Dirty Bertie

Uh-oh. What was that? Bertie turned round slowly. A giant dog stood there, growling at him. It was the biggest dog he'd ever seen – bigger than a wolf. Its ears were folded back and its fur stood on end. Bertie gulped. It looked like the kind of dog that ate paper boys for breakfast.

"Good dog," he squeaked. "I won't hurt you."

"GRRRRRR… RUFF!" barked the dog. It was wearing a collar with the name "Brutus" in big letters.

"Stay, Brutus, stay," said Bertie. "I'm just going to put this paper through the letterbox, okay?"

He bent down slowly to take a newspaper from the bag. Brutus snarled, showing rows of sharp white teeth. "GRRR!"

Bertie dropped the paper and flew back over the wall, landing in a heap.

What now? This was impossible! How was he meant to deliver the paper with a giant dog trying to eat him alive?

CHAPTER 3

Bertie stood outside the gate of number twenty-two wondering what to do.

At last Darren appeared.

"What are you waiting for?" he said. "I thought we were in a hurry!"

"Never mind that," said Bertie. "There's a dog at this house."

"Oh no, NOT A DOG!" cried

Dirty Bertie

Darren, pretending to tremble. "Did the nasty doggy bark at you?"

Bertie scowled. "It's a monster," he said. "I was lucky to get out alive."

Darren shrugged. "Well, as long as you delivered the paper."

"How could I?" said Bertie. "He wouldn't let me near the door."

Darren was frowning at him. "Where's your bag?" he asked.

"What?"

"The bag – with all the newspapers," said Darren.

Bertie turned round. ARGH! In his panic he must have left the bag in the driveway!

"You didn't leave it?" groaned Darren.

"It's not my fault!" said Bertie. "He was after me!"

Dirty Bertie

"But we've still got the other houses to do," said Darren. "You'll have to go back."

"Are you MAD?" cried Bertie. "Go in there?"

"It's only a dog!" said Darren. "Don't be such a baby!"

Bertie dragged Darren to the gate and pointed down the drive. Brutus was tearing a newspaper to shreds with his teeth.

"*That's* what I'm talking about," said Bertie.

"Yikes," gasped Darren. "He's ENORMOUS!"

"I know," said Bertie. "But like you say, he's only a dog, so why don't *you* get the bag?"

"No way!" said Darren. "You're the one who left it."

They stared through the gate.

Now what? thought Bertie. Without the bag they didn't have enough papers to finish the round. The shop would get complaints and Neil would hear about it. Worst of all, they wouldn't get paid. There was only one thing for it — someone had to face Brutus.

CHAPTER 4

Bertie's hands were damp with sweat. He grasped the gate. This was it, he was probably going to die. Tomorrow morning his parents would read about it in the newspaper – though not if it wasn't delivered.

"Take a stick," suggested Darren.

"To fight him off?" said Bertie.

"No dumbo, for him to fetch," said Darren. "When he runs after it you can grab the bag."

Bertie nodded. It was worth a try. Whiffer could never resist a stick so Brutus was probably the same. Bertie found a stick in someone's front garden. Actually it was more like a twig, but it was the best he could do.

Opening the gate, he tiptoed inside. The gate swung slowly back into place.

CLANG!

Bertie groaned. There went any chance of sneaking in quietly.

"Hurry up!" hissed Darren.

Bertie crept down the drive. "Don't panic, keep calm," he said to himself. His dad said that dogs could smell fear.

"Hi! Me again," croaked Bertie. Brutus

rose to his feet. He seemed to have grown even bigger since last time.

"Look – STICK!" cried Bertie, holding out the twig. "You like sticks, eh?"

Brutus's tail thumped against the wall. Bertie took a step closer, breathing hard. This was near enough. He drew back his arm and threw the stick, which landed on the lawn.

"FETCH BOY! FETCH!" cried Bertie.

Brutus turned his head, considering whether it was worth the effort.

It was now or never. Bertie darted forward and grabbed the bag of papers. Brutus snarled. Suddenly he sprang forward, seizing one of the bag straps.

Help! thought Bertie, trying to pull the

bag away.

Brutus pulled back.

"LET GO!" grunted Bertie.

"GRRR! GRRR!"

Suddenly there was a loud ripping sound as the strap came away. Bertie fell back on the drive with the bag on top of him. Newspapers flew everywhere. He felt hot smelly breath on his face and got a close-up of Brutus's teeth.

This is it, thought Bertie. *I'm dead...*

"BRUTUS! COME HERE!"

Bertie opened his eyes and sat up. A man had come out of the house. Brutus bounded over to him, wagging his tail.

"It's okay, he won't hurt you!" said the man. "He's just a big softie."

You could have fooled me, thought Bertie.

The man looked around. Bits of
newspaper littered his garden. One
page was caught in a rose bush.

"You're not the usual paper boy, are
you?" he said.

"Oh no. This is my first day," grunted
Bertie, getting to his feet.

"So I see," said the man. "Looks like
you need a bit more practice."

Dirty Bertie

About an hour later, Neil called round
to pay them their money.

"Everything go okay?" he asked. "You
get rid of all the papers?"

"Oh yes," said Bertie. They'd certainly
got rid of them all, though not always
through a letterbox. To get
back in time for *Danny's Deadly
Dinosaurs* they'd had to
finish in a hurry.

Dirty Bertie

"We ran into a bit of trouble," said Bertie. "At number twenty-two."

Neil laughed. "Ah right, you met Brutus then?"

"You know him?" said Darren.

"I should do, he's chased me often enough," said Neil, grinning at them. "Why do you think I gave you Hazel Road?"

Bertie couldn't believe it. Neil had known about Brutus from the start and he hadn't even warned them. No wonder he wanted to get rid of half his paper round!

"Anyway, no harm done," said Neil, handing them fifty pence each. "So same time next week then?"

Bertie and Darren looked at each other.

Dirty Bertie

"No thanks," said Bertie.

Neil's grin vanished. "But what about our deal – a pound a week?" he said.

"That's okay, you keep it," said Bertie. "Oh, and say hi to Brutus for me."

Bertie closed the front door. Next time he wanted a job he'd look for something safer – lion taming for instance.

Dirty Bertie

"I'm saving up for a new bike."

"I'm buying a telescope," said Bertie.
"Look, isn't that him?"

Neil came out of school, swinging his
bag. He stopped when he saw them and
listened as they explained their idea.

"A paper round? You two?" Neil laughed, shaking his head. "You've got to be thirteen at least."

"We could look thirteen," said Bertie. "Especially if we wear false beards."

"Yeah, good one!" grinned Neil. "Anyway there's nothing going, all the paper rounds are taken."

"Are you sure?" asked Darren.

"I should know," said Neil. "I had to wait six months to get one."

Bertie and Darren looked disappointed. They had raised their hopes for nothing. Now they'd never earn any money. They turned to go – but Neil stopped them.

"Tell you what," he said. "Where do you live?"

"Me? Fleaman Drive," said Bertie.